LITTLE BAT
up all day

CALDECOTT HONOR WINNER AND *NEW YORK TIMES* BESTSELLER
BRIAN LIES

CLARION BOOKS
An Imprint of HarperCollinsPublishers
BOSTON   NEW YORK

For my sister Elaine, who lives a half day ahead of me, on Tokyo time

Clarion Books is an imprint of HarperCollins Publishers.

Little Bat Up All Day
Copyright © 2022 by Brian Lies
All rights reserved. No part of this book may be used or reproduced in any manner whatsoever without written permission
except in the case of brief quotations embodied in critical articles and reviews. For information address HarperCollins
Children's Books, a division of HarperCollins Publishers, 195 Broadway, New York, NY 10007.
clarionbooks.com

The Library of Congress Cataloging-in-Publication Data is on file.

The illustrations in this book were done with acrylic and
watercolor paints and colored pencil on Strathmore paper.
The text was set in Adobe Garamond Pro.
Design by Natalie Fondriest

ISBN: 978-0-358-26985-4

Manufactured in Italy
RTLO 10 9 8 7 6 5 4 3 2 1
4500846038

First Edition

"What's daytime like?" Little Bat asked as the sun rose.

"It's brighter and noisier," Mama Bat said. "Otherwise, it's the same—just animals going about their lives."

"But different animals?" Little Bat asked.

"Yes," Mama replied. "Ones that sleep at *night*."

"Can I stay up to meet them?" he asked.

Mama smiled. "We need rest so we can fly at night."

As Little Bat's family drifted off to sleep,
his mind raced. He *had* to know what the
daytime was like and who was out there.

He poked his head outside. Everything seemed so
strange, and questions buzzed in his head.

Are the trees in different places during the day?

Will the sun hurt my eyes?

What happened to the stars?

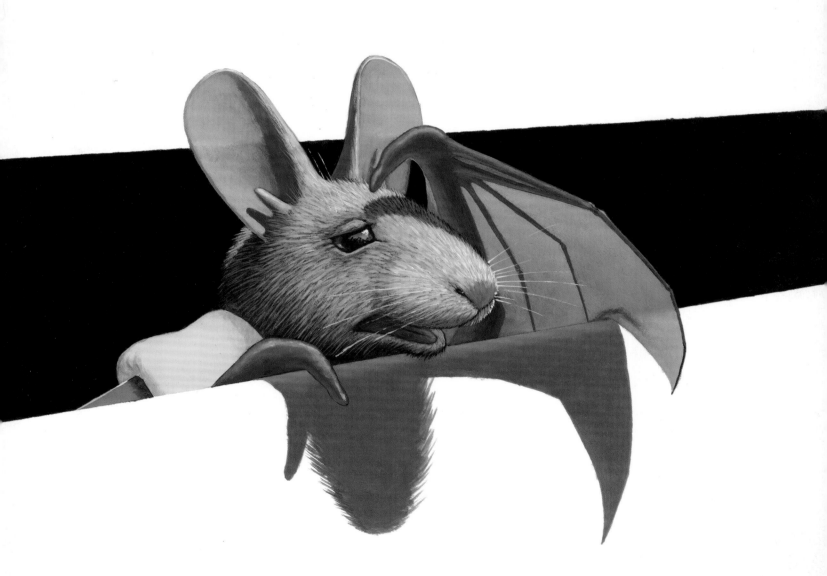

He leapt out into the air,

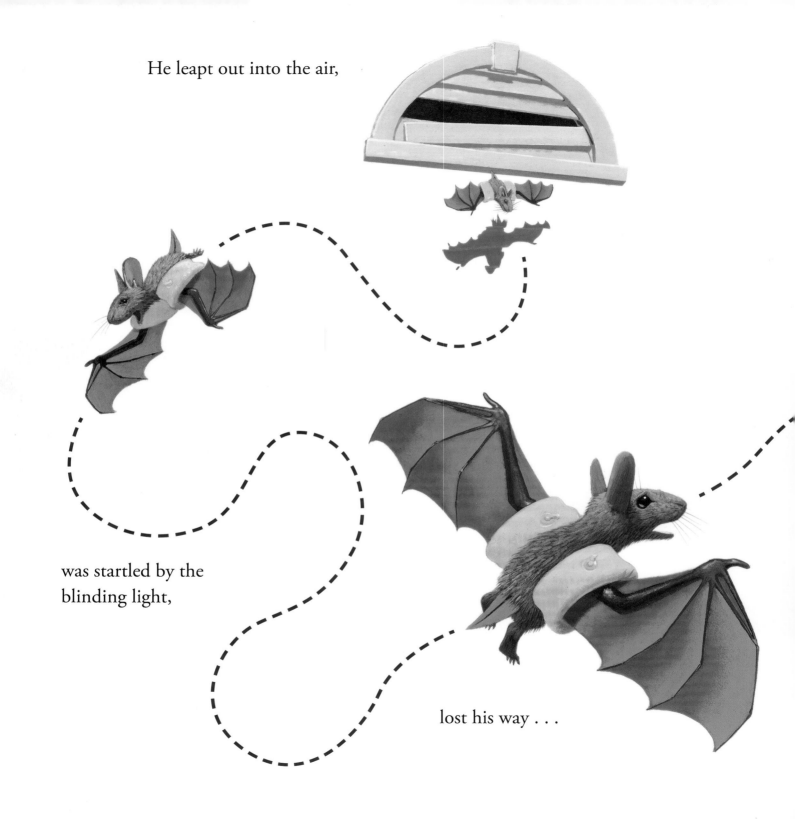

was startled by the
blinding light,

lost his way . . .

. . . and found a tree.

OOF

Breathing hard, he scrambled onto
a branch. Everything was loud and
bright and confusing.
Where am I?
Where is home?
Will I ever get back?

Then Little Bat closed his eyes.
"Too much!"
      He chirped loudly—

—and laughed with relief. The echo that bounced back painted a soothing picture in his brain. He heard *exactly* where he was— right in his own backyard.

When he glanced up, he saw a magnificent bird
sailing across the sky.

    Maybe they could be friends! Little Bat waved.

OOF! Somebody knocked him off the branch and pulled him under a bench.

"What were you doing?!" the squirrel gasped. "That was a hawk. A hawk! It might have gotten you!"

Little Bat shivered. He'd heard about hawks.

The squirrel exhaled. "It's gone now. Gone! I'm Rusty. You aren't from around here, are you?" she asked.

"I live here," he said. "I'm Little Bat. I'm usually not awake now, but I'm happy to meet you. I'm staying up *all day*."

Rusty laughed. "I do that all the time. All the time."

"Well, have you ever stayed up all night?" Little Bat asked.

Rusty paused. "I tried once. Tried! Kept falling asleep."

"*I'm* not going to fall asleep," Little Bat said. "I'm going to watch the sun go down."

"Maybe I can help keep you awake," Rusty said. "Follow me."

Rusty was quick. Little Bat had to fly fast to keep up with her.

"Try this," Rusty said.

Little Bat took a nibble. It was slimy and tasted like dirt.

"These *are* kind of sticky," Rusty said. "I like to wash in the fountain after eating."

"We *love* the fountain!" Little Bat said.

"Bats know about the fountain?" Rusty asked, amazed.

They splashed in the water for a while.

But the warm sun made Little Bat feel drowsy.

"Wake up, Little Bat!" Rusty poked him.

"I wasn't sleeping," Little Bat protested. "I was just resting my eyes." He shook his head to clear it. "Let's try something else!"

There were lots of fun things
to do together in the yard.

Soccer wasn't one of them.

Late in the morning, they discovered a place that hadn't
been used for a long time.

"This could make a great clubhouse," Little Bat said.

They got to work cleaning
and decorating.

Rusty tapped a gavel. "I call this meeting to ord—"

She laughed. "Wake up, Little Bat.
You're sleeping again. Sleeping!"

"I *wasn't* sleeping! I was just imagining
what sleeping here would be like. Let's
go out into the sunlight."

They made shadows in the bright sunshine.

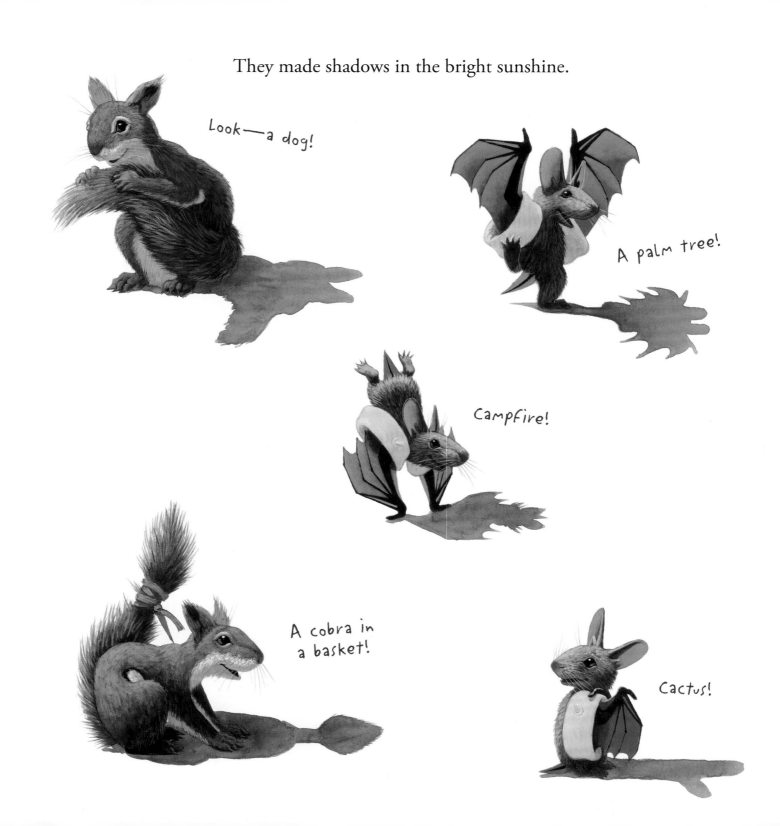

Look—a dog!

A palm tree!

Campfire!

A cobra in a basket!

Cactus!

Look—a snowman!

. . . Little Bat?

Wake up, Little Bat!
Wake up!
Wake up!

"Arrgh!" Little Bat wailed. "I can't do it. I *was* sleeping. I didn't even make it to *noon!*"

Rusty frowned. "You sleep during the day, and I sleep at night. How can we stay friends if we can't even *be* together?"

"I don't think we can," Little Bat sighed. "But this was so much fun."

They said goodbye, and Little Bat flapped back up to the attic to get the rest he desperately needed.

That night, he went back to the clubhouse.
It felt very empty without Rusty.

So he scratched a note to her,
hoping she would find it.

The next night, there was a
note waiting for him . . .

. . . and Little Bat realized that they *could* stay friends after all.